Rosie & Jim
Jim Gets Lost

By John Cunliffe Illustrated by Joan and Jane Hickson

A Ragdoll Production for Central Independent Television

Hippo

Scholastic Children's Books,
Scholastic Publications Ltd,
7-9 Pratt Street, London NW1 0AE

Scholastic Inc.,
730 Broadway, New York, NY 10003, USA

Scholastic Canada Ltd,
123 Newkirk Road, Richmond Hill,
Ontario, Canada L4C 3G5

Ashton Scholastic Pty Ltd,
PO Box 579, Gosford, New South Wales,
Australia

Ashton Scholastic Ltd,
Private Bag 1, Penrose, Auckland,
New Zealand

First published by Scholastic Publication Ltd. 1993

Based on the Central Independent Television
series produced by Ragdoll Productions

ISBN: 0 590 54104 8

Typeset by Rapid Reprographics
Printed in Hong Kong by the Paramount Printing Group

Rosie and Jim were going along
the canal on the good boat,
Ragdoll. They looked out of the
window to see what they could see.

3

"Look!" said Rosie. "There's a cloud sitting on a hill."

"Ooooh," said Jim. "I'm going to climb up that hill and see the cloud."

"Noggin," said Rosie,"you can see clouds any day, up in the sky."

"But I want to see one close to. I want to touch it, and see what it looks like inside."

"Fizzy-noggin," said Rosie. "Well,
then, bring a piece back for me."

"Aren't you coming?"

"No, I'm not," said Rosie, "I'm
busy with my painting."

So Jim had to go by himself. He took an empty jar with him, so that he could bring a piece of cloud back for Rosie.

Jim climbed up the hill. It was a
long way and he was soon out of
puff. He sat down for a rest. How
far away the *Ragdoll* was now and
how little it looked. Jim set off
again.

He was getting close to the top now. Jim could see the hill going up into the cloud. Soon he would be able to touch it.

"I wonder what it's made of?" said Jim to himself. "It looks like fluffy cotton-wool."

As Jim climbed up, things began to change. The sun stopped shining. All went cold and clammy, misty and damp. Jim couldn't see the cloud now. He couldn't see much at

all. There was a white something
all round him. The trees, and the
cows, and the sheep kept going
away into this cold wet white stuff,
then coming back again. He kept
walking into things.

13

"Ooooops! Help!" shouted Jim. He had fallen over a monster with long horns. It was only a sheep, lying in the grass. It jumped up and ran off into the whiteness.

"I think I'll go home."

But which was the way home? He looked all about him, but he could not see the *Ragdoll* now. He could only see this white stuff all round him. Jim was lost in a very thick fog!

"I think *this* is the way."

He set out, walking quickly. Too quickly. "Oooops! Help!"

There was a splash and a squelch of mud. "I never saw that before! I must be going the wrong way! Oh, deary me, I wish I'd never come."

This way and that way Jim walked,
but he could not find his way
home. Then he saw something
peeping over the top of a wall. "It's
the *Ragdoll's* chimney. It must be!"

Jim climbed over the wall. "Oh!"
It was an old tractor, with its
exhaust pipe sticking up in the fog,
just like the chimney on the
Ragdoll.

Jim set off again.

Could that be Rosie, standing
behind that bush? It looked just like
her mop of hair in the foggy
whiteness.

"Rosie! Rosie!"

Jim ran towards the bush. "Oh!"

It was a mop that someone had
left leaning against a gate-post. It
looked just like Rosie's hair.

Poor Jim! He felt so sad and so lost.
It was too cold and wet to stay
where he was, so he set out again,
walking into the whiteness all
around him.

Then he saw a sight that made him
feel happy.

"Fizzgog!"

There was John, standing very
still in the middle of the field, with
his old straw hat on his head and
his back to Jim.

"I'd know that hat anywhere,"
said Jim.

He ran towards John. He would
surely lead him back to the *Ragdoll*.

"I expect he's come to see the cloud so that he can put it in a story," said Jim.

Jim came closer and closer to John. John didn't move at all. He was as still as a statue. Jim came

right up to him. What had happened to John's feet? They had turned into sticks that were stuck into the ground. Jim walked round in front of John. "Oh!"

John's face was made of an old
sack filled with straw with buttons
sewn on for eyes, a stick for a nose
and a line of stitches for a mouth. It
wasn't John at all. It was a
scarecrow. And *he* couldn't tell Jim
the way home. Poor old Jim! He
didn't know what to do. He sat
down by the scarecrow and
hugged himself to keep warm and
wondered what to do.

Then Jim heard something. Very
faint, but a sound he knew.
  Quack!
  That must be Duck. Even if it
wasn't the *Ragdoll's* very own
Duck, it was still a duck. And ducks
live on water. So...

Jim stood up and listened very
hard. There it was again. It was
one thing the fog could not hide.

Quack! Quack!

"It's coming from that way. That's
the way I'll go."

Jim followed the Quacks.

Quack!

Louder and louder came the sound of Duck. Over walls and through bushes Jim followed the sound. He walked through a stream and a muddy bog. He stepped in some nettles. But Jim did not stop. He followed the sounds, until he came out of the fog.

RAGDOLL

The sun was shining again. And there was the *Ragdoll* right in front of him with Duck on the roof and Rosie in the cabin. How glad he was to see them!

"Thanks, Duck, for quacking me home!" called Jim.

He ran to Rosie, and she gave him a great big hug.

"Oh, Rosie, Rosie..." said Jim, and he told her all about his adventure.

RAGDOLL

"Ooh, noggin," said Rosie, "my hair *doesn't* look like a mop!"

"In the middle of a cloud," said Jim, "anything can look like anything."

"And did you bring me my jar of cloud?" said Rosie.

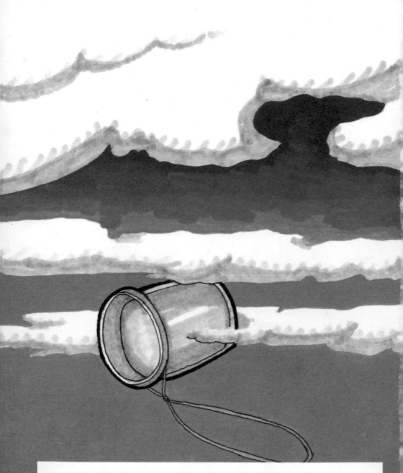

But Jim couldn't find that jar
anywhere.
    "It's lost in the fog," he said. "And
it can't be quacked home."